D0519890

MAGGIE and HERO

written by Margaret O'Brien

illustrated by Veselina Tomova

Fineday Books

St. John's, Newfoundland and Labrador

Text copyright © 2006 by Margaret O'Brien
Illustrations copyright © 2006 by Veselina Tomova

All rights reserved. No part of this publication may be reproduced, transmitted in any form
or by any means, electronic, mechanical, photocopying, or otherwise, or stored in a retrieval system,
without the prior written consent of Fineday Books—or in the case of photocopying or other
reprographic copying, a license from the Canadian Copyright Licensing Agency (Access Copyright).
For an Access Copyright License, visit www.accesscopyright.com or call toll free to 1-800-893-5777.

Published in Canada by Fineday Books,
P.O. Box 1145, Stn. C, St. John's, NL, A1C 5M5
www.finedaybooks.ca

Design and layout by vis-à-vis graphics inc.
www.visavisgraphics.com

Library and Archives Canada Cataloguing in Publication
O'Brien, Margaret, date.
     Maggie and Hero / Margaret O'Brien ; Veselina Tomova, illustrator.
ISBN 0-9699530-1-1
     1. Dogs--Juvenile fiction. I. Tomova, Veselina, 1958- II. Title.
PS8629.B729M35 2006   jC813'.6   C2006-900590-7

First printed in Canada, 2006
Printed and bound in China, 2007

to Lena and Dan O'Brien
for the gift, and Heather and Alex
for the fun
M.O.B.

to Kokich,
Doggie and Puppsy
for being my best boys
V.T.

Oh dear. I don't like that finger, thought Maggie.

I don't know why everybody is so angry with me.

I really don't.

I wanted to say hello to all those nice people at the birthday party. I wanted to bounce that beautiful beach ball just once. But the ball was too bouncy, and the table got in the way.

It really wasn't my fault!

Well, it was a birthday party, so I thought that
I could have just a teeny piece of cake. **But it all
got stuck in my teeth!**

I just wanted to give that little boy a hug and a kiss for his birthday. But he wasn't very happy about that.

I liked him **SOOOO** much. I don't know why he didn't like me.

Everyone is so angry with me.

They say that I'm too big.

They say my paws are too clumsy.

They say my tail is too long and wavy.

I can't do anything right.

But I must be good for something!

I'm going to find out what it is, and then I'll show them.

OOOOOH

It's the boy's beautiful birthday beach ball. The cats have stolen it.

BAD CATS!!!!

I'm going to take that ball away from those cats and give it back to the boy. Maybe then he'll like me!

Oh no! I wanted to give
the ball back to the boy.
And now I'm trapped here.
The wind is too pushy,
and the sea is so choppy,
and I don't know how to swim!
And here come those bad cats
to steal the ball back again.
There must be
a hundred of them.

And there's
only
one
of me.

"Hello, puppy," said the giant.
"My name is Hero. Let's get you out of here
before those cats land on you."

"Could you?" gasped Maggie.
"Would you really?"

"Certainly," said Hero. "Delighted to help, I'm sure."

With that, Hero picked Maggie up by the loose fur
at the back of her neck and tossed her into the small
bouncing boat.

"This is a very rocky boat," gasped Maggie.

"And by the way, my name is not 'puppy.'
It's Maggie."

"Pleased to meet you," said Hero. "I'd rather not meet
those cats though, Maggie. So let's get out of here."

"What is that noise?" asked Maggie, sneezing and shaking water all over Hero.

"That's the rescue bell," said Hero. "Someone has fallen into the sea. Let's see if we can help."

"Maybe you can help," said Maggie,
"But I can't swim,
and I'm not good at anything.
Wait a minute—what's that over
there in the water?"

"Over where?" asked Hero. "Oh, I
see now. You have very sharp eyes,
Maggie, and that's very useful.
There's a boy in the water. It looks
as though he's in trouble."

"It's the boy from the birthday party," said Maggie. "What shall we do? **Oh no! The beach ball has bounced into the water!**"

"Good," said Hero.

"Why 'good'?" asked Maggie.

"The boy can hold onto the ball, and you can pull him into the boat. He knows you."

"He doesn't like me," cried Maggie.

"He will like you when you pull him out of the water," said Hero.

WHOOOOOSH

"I CAN'T! I can't swim!!!!" gasped Maggie.

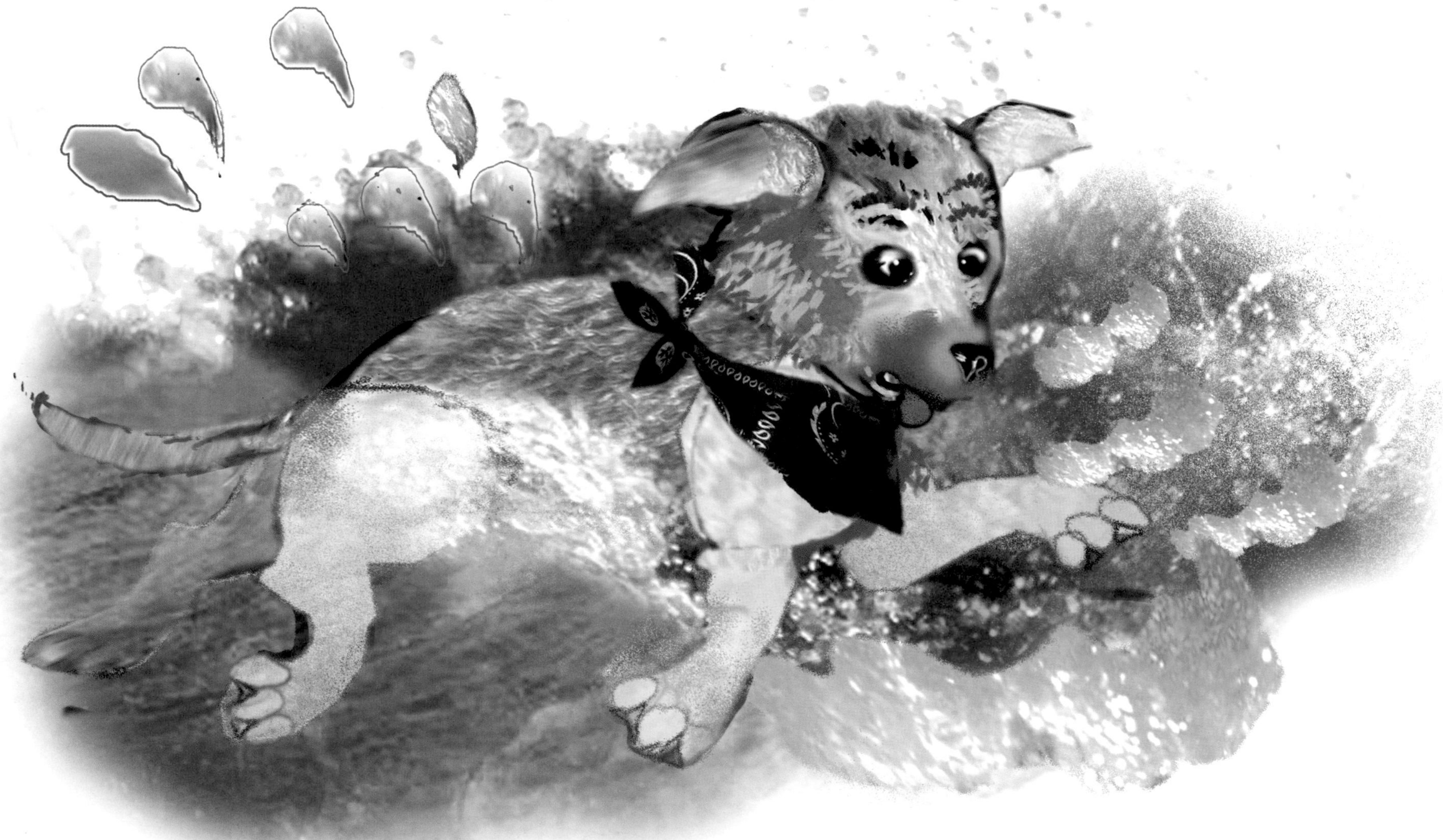

"Yes, you can,"
called Hero.

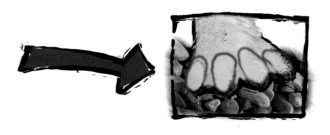

"Use your paws, Maggie.
That's what they're made for.

"Steer with your tail.

"Your fur will keep you warm.

"You're a water dog, Maggie.
You just didn't know it."

Ahhh, thought Maggie. Perhaps Hero is right. Perhaps I am a water dog. My big **paws** paddle. My **tail** steers me where I want to go. My **fur** stays nice and dry. My **jaws** are good for pulling things along in the water. Come on, boy. Don't struggle. Let me do all the work.

"Why are all these people here?" asked Maggie.
"What are they doing?"

"It looks like they're going to have a parade," said Hero.

"Oh fun!" said Maggie. "What's the parade for?"

"For you, Maggie," said Hero. "It's for you!"

"Me? But why?"

"Because you saved the boy. The townspeople
want to say thank you."

"Are you sure?" asked Maggie. "I wasn't very popular
at the birthday party."

"Well, that was then, and this is now, Maggie," said Hero.

"Come on, Maggie," nudged Hero. "Smile for the cameras. How does it feel to be famous?"

"A bit silly, really," said Maggie. "Is my fur smooth? Are my ears up? Should I let them see my teeth? What do you think?"

Hero laughed. "I think you're **the best looking water dog I've ever seen**."

"Hurry now! It's your parade, and they can't start without you.
Do you hear? The band has started to play."

Down the street went the parade. Maggie's tail wagged,
her paws pounced, and her fur shone in the sunlight.

The whole town laughed as she skipped up the street.

A whole lot can happen in a day, thought Maggie.

This morning when I woke up, everyone said
I was a nuisance, and I thought I would be sad
forever and ever.

Now it's almost bedtime, and so much has happened.
I met my friend Hero and the one hundred cats.
I learned to swim and saved the boy from the sea.
I had my own parade, and now I'm watching
the fireworks.

I don't feel sad any more.
I feel glad.

I do feel sleepy though.
It's been a long day
for this small
water dog.